Millions of Americans remember Dick and Jane (and Sally and Spot too!). The little stories with their simple vocabulary words and warmly rendered illustrations were a hallmark of American education in the 1950s and 1960s.

But the first Dick and Jane stories actually appeared much earlier—in the Scott Foresman Elson Basic Reader Pre-Primer, copyright 1930. These books featured short, upbeat, and highly readable stories for children. The pages were filled with colorful characters and large, easy-to-read Century Schoolbook typeface. There were fun adventures around every corner of Dick and Jane's world.

Generations of American children learned to read with Dick and Jane, and many still cherish the memory of reading the simple stories on their own. Today, Pearson Scott Foresman remains committed to helping all children learn to read—and love to read. As part of Pearson Education, the world's largest educational publisher, Pearson Scott Foresman is honored to reissue these classic Dick and Jane stories, with Grosset & Dunlap, a division of Penguin Young Readers Group. Reading has always been at the heart of everything we do, and we sincerely hope that reading is an important part of your life too.

Library of Congress Cataloging-in-Publication Data is available.

ISBN 0-448-43402-4 (pbk)   B C D E F G H I J
ISBN 0-448-43414-8 (GB)   B C D E F G H I J

Read with
Dick and Jane

Jump and Run

GROSSET & DUNLAP • NEW YORK

Puff

Jump, Puff.

Jump, jump, jump.

Jump, Puff, jump.

Run, Puff.

Run, Puff, run.

Run, run, run.

Jump, jump, jump.

Oh, Puff.

Oh, oh, oh.

Funny, funny Puff.

Spot

Come, come.

Come, Spot, come.

Run, run, run.

Jump, Spot.

Jump, jump.

Jump, Spot, jump.

Oh, Spot.

Oh, oh, oh.

Funny, funny Spot.

Jump and Play

Sally said, "Oh, look.
Mother can jump.
Mother can jump and play."

Dick said, "Jump, Father.
You can jump.
You can jump and play."

"Look, Mother," said Sally.
"See Father jump.
See Father jump and play.
Big, big Father is funny."

Jane said, "Oh, Father.
You can not jump and play.
Spot can not jump and play."

Dick said, "Oh, see Puff.
Puff can jump.
Puff can jump and play."

Run and Help

Run, Jane.

Help Mother.

Run, Jane, run.

Help Mother work.

Come, Sally, come.

Come and help.

Come and help Mother.

Run, run, run.

Look, Sally, look.

See Spot work.

Funny, funny Spot.

Oh, oh, oh.

Spot can help Mother.

See Puff Jump

Look, Dick.

See Puff jump.

Oh, look.

Look and see.

See Puff jump and play.

Come, Jane, come.

Come and see Puff.

See Puff jump and run.

See funny, little Puff.

Oh, oh, oh.

See little Puff run.

Oh, see Puff.

Funny, little Puff.

Spot and Tim and Puff

Spot can jump.

Little Puff can jump.

Look, Tim, look.

See Spot and Puff play.

Look, Tim.

See Sally jump.

See Sally jump down.

Down, down, down.

Sally can jump and play.

Oh, Puff.

See funny, little Tim.

See Tim jump down.

Down, down, down.

Tim can jump and play.

Oh, See

Look, Sally, look.

Look down.

Look down, Sally.

Look down, down, down.

Look up, Sally.

Look up, up, up.

Run, Sally, run.

Run and jump.

Run and jump up.

Look, Jane.

Look and see.

Oh, see.

See funny, funny Sally.